Nevada Native Americans

A Kid's Look at Our State's Chiefs, Tribes, Reservations, Powwows, Lore, and More From The Past and the Present

By Carole Marsh

Native American Heritage™

Graphic Design: Lynette Rowe • Cover Design: Victoria DeJoy

NATIVE AMERICAN HERITAGE™

CAROLE MARSH BOOKS

Published by
GALLOPADE™ INTERNATIONAL
800-536-2GET
www.gallopade.com

Gallopade is proud to be a member of these educational organizations and associations:

The National School Supply and Equipment Association (NSSEA)
American Booksellers Association (ABA)
Virginia Educational Media Association (VEMA)
Association of Partners for Public Lands (APPL)
Museum Store Association (MSA)
National Association for Gifted Children (NAGC)
Publishers Marketing Association (PMA)
International Reading Association (IRA)
Association of African American Museums (AAAM)

Native American Heritage™ Series

Native American Big Activity Book

Native American Biographies

Native American Coloring Book

Native American Heritage Book

Native American Timeline

Nevada State Stuff™

- My First Pocket Guide: Nevada
- My First Book About Nevada
- Nevada Coloring Book
- The Big Nevada Reproducible Activity Book
- Jeopardy: Answers & Questions About Our State
- Nevada "Jography!": A Fun Run Through Our State
- Nevada Gamebooks
- Nevada Bingo Games
- Nevada Illustrated Timelines
- Nevada Project Books
- Nevada Bulletin Board Set
- Nevada PosterMap
- Nevada Stickers
- Let's Discover Nevada! CD-ROM

Word from the Author

Hello!

I hope you are as interested in North America's wonderful Indian heritage as I am!

Like most kids, I grew up thinking of Indians as the other half of Cowboys. Today, of course, we are getting a much clearer and more accurate picture of what the first peoples on our land were all about. These "facts" are much more fascinating than anything Hollywood can make up. And you probably won't find much of this information in your history textbook!

I am 1/16 Cherokee. This is something I am very proud of and happy about. My grandmother was 1/4 Cherokee. She had tan skin, long gray hair and a very Indian look – especially if I did something bad! Her maiden name was Carrie Corn. Of course, when she got married, she took her husband's name, so it was many years before I learned to appreciate the significance of my native heritage.

Today, I'm trying to make up for lost time by exploring my roots as deeply as I can. One of the most interesting things I've learned is how fascinating all of the Indian tribes are – in the past, the present and future!

As you read about "your" Indians, remember that all native peoples were part of an ever-changing network of time, ideas, power and luck — good and bad. This is certainly a history that is not "dead," but continues to change – often right outside our own back doors! – all the time.

Carole Marsh
She-Who-Writes

PS: Many references show different spellings for the same word. I have tried to select the most common spelling for the time period described. I would not want to be in an Indian spelling bee!

A is for . . .

Adobe

Brick made of mud plus straw and dried in the sun. Houses made of adobe are cool inside, even in high temperatures, because the walls are so thick.

Awl

An Indian's "needle." Often made from wood, thorns, bone, or metal, it was used to punch holes in skins so they could be sewn together.

Adze

An Indian woodworking tool used to cut, scrape, or gouge; often used to hollow dugout canoes. Blades were made of stone, shell, bone or copper.

Anasazi

Early Nevada people whose name means "the ancient ones." Lived in simple pit houses in the Moapa Valley around B.C. 500. They made beautiful pottery. Around 500 A.D. they mined salt and turquoise to trade with their neighbors. After A.D. 700 built dams on the Virgin and Muddy rivers to store water and became Nevada's first farmers, growing cotton, corn, beans and squash. Some built adobe pueblos which often had 100 rooms! Since their paintings do not show warfare, they probably lived in peace with their neighbors.

Agaihtikara

Indians who lived near the Walker and Carson Rivers in Nevada. Called the "fish eaters." Numbered about 1,500 Indians. Active around 1866. Ruled by Chief Oderie.

Altar

A platform made of rocks or animal skulls; some had bowls, feathers, rattles, or skins on them. Indians prayed at these altars for things like good crops or expert hunting skills.

Arrow

A long, slender shaft made of reed, cane, or wood; pointed tip was attached to one end and split feathers to the other. Feathers helped the arrows fly straight.

Arrowhead

The pointed tip of an arrow, made of bone, antler, wood, or iron. Some tips had barbs that would embed themselves in flesh. These barbs made it difficult for an enemy to remove the arrowhead from a wound.

Aborigine

A member of the earliest known population of a region.

Archaeology

Excavations from Nevada sites indicate that native peoples lived here 12,000 years ago. Archaeologists have unearthed their remains, as well as the bones of extinct horses, camels and elephants.

B is for . . .

Balsa

A type of boat or raft made by tying bundles of rushes together in a cigar shape. Also made of tule grass on Pyramid Lake in Nevada.

Band

A subdivision of an Indian tribe. In earlier times, a band was sometimes created when part of a tribe split off from the main group. The band also chose new leadership.

Blankets

Used for door covers, partitions, bags, to dry food on, carry babies and many other purposes.

Baskets

Made from roots, grasses, barks and other natural materials. Some were woven, others coiled. Basketwork made by Nevada Indians was also used for fences, fish nets, houses, mats, shields, cradles and other items. The Washoe Indians were outstanding basket makers.

Bullroarer

Sacred instrument symbolizing rain, lightning and thunder. Made of a rectangular piece of wood and a cord. The wood is pine or fir and should come from trees that have been struck by lightning. A person would twirl the wooden part above the head, holding onto the cord.

Buckskin

Softened, smoke-treated rawhide. Used by Nevada Indians to make clothes, bags and pouches.

Bow

Made from wood, horn or bone. Nevada Indian children learned how to use bows. The bowstring was made from animal gut, rawhide or twisted vegetable fibers.

Bone

Animal bones were used by Nevada Indians to make buttons, whistles and other items.

Beads

Made of wood, shells, claws, minerals, seeds — you name it! Later, the Nevada Indians traded with white men for glass beads, used in some of their decorative arts.

C is for . . .

Chief

Leader of a tribe. Different titles meant different things. Some members were made chief because they owned deeds to land. Chieftainship was often inherited, usually from the mother!

Canoe

The Indians invented this useful boat. The "rough" side of the canoe was on the outside, not the inside!

Contact Period

What historians call the era in the 1500s when Native Americans first met Europeans. This meeting changed the lifestyle of the Nevada Indians more than anyone could ever have anticipated!

Can You Hear the Message?

The Ghost Dance Religion spread among the Plains Tribes in the 1880s. It centered around returning to native ways and living together in harmony. It preached that the earth would soon die, to come alive again for only the Indians. The religion called for ridding oneself of the white ways, prayer, meditation, chanting and dancing – particularly the Ghost Dance. Founded by a Nevada Northern Paiute named Wovoka (also known as Jack Wilson).

Citizenship

The Indian Citizenship Act of 1924 states all Indians born in the United States are citizens of the United States, and citizens of the states they live in, even though they may live on a reservation. They can vote. They pay most local, state and federal taxes, including sales taxes.

Confederacy

A union of different groups of people. A confederacy in Indian culture was a group of tribes that agreed not to fight with each other. They agreed to live peacefully. Sometimes the tribes shared culture and language.

Comstock Problem

Nevada's early Indians were upset at how their lives were disrupted after gold was discovered on Mount Davidson in 1859. The mine was named after one of its owners.

Crops

: The Mojave farmed the flood plains of the Colorado River. They grey corn, beans, wheat, melons, and even pumpkins!

Clan

A tribal unit. Members are descended from the same ancestor.

D is for . . .

Dance

There were Indian dances for every occasion: war, peace, hunting, rain, good harvests, etc. Drums, rattles, and flutes of bone or reed provided the music. Dancers often chanted or sang while performing. Steps were not easy to learn and required consistent practice.

Descendants

The first Nevada Indians were descendants of primitive hunters who crossed the Bering Strait from Asia to what is now Alaska. At that time, glacial ice still covered most of North America. These people were the true discoverers of the "New World!"

Disease

Nevada Indians had no immunity to the diseases that white explorers, colonists and settlers brought to their lands. These diseases included smallpox, measles, tuberculosis and others, which ravaged the tribes in great epidemics that killed many, and sometimes all, members of a tribe.

Dat-So-La-Lee

One of the most notable Washoe Indian basket makers. Her works of art are prized by modern collectors and the Nevada state legislature passed a law to preserve her work. She is credited with single-handedly changing Washoe basket weaving. She also created a new shape of basket called degikup, a new dye, and influenced the new curio style and the three-coil method.

Dyes

Made of lichens, berries, roots, bark, plants, and other natural materials by Indians in Nevada. Different colors were used depending on what materials were available and what objects were to be dyed.

Darts

Rock hunters in Nevada have found stone dart points that are 10,000 years old, which were used by Stone Age peoples for hunting before the bow and arrow were invented.

Dr. Carlos Montezuma

Full-blooded Apache who grew up in the wild but graduated from medical school and served as a doctor at the Western Shoshone Agency in Nevada.

Dreams

Important in the Indian tradition. It was believed that dreams were the "windows" to the soul. Many thought a person's hidden desires were expressed in dreams.

E is for . . .

Eagle

An animal used in many Indian ceremonies. Eagle feathers attached to war bonnets and shields communicated an Indian's rank in his tribe and what kinds of deeds he had done. Feathers also adorned rattles, pipes, baskets, and prayer sticks.

Everyone Should Visit

These Nevada Indian attractions: Nevada State Museum, Carson City; Stewart Indian Museum, Carson City; Northeastern Nevada Museum, Elko; Lost City Museum, Overton; Numana Hatchery Visitors Center, Wadsworth.

Earrings

Medicine men sometimes pierced male and female ears at special ceremonies. Earrings, which cost parents or relatives a significant amount, symbolized wealth and distinction. The more earrings that an Indian wore, the greater his honor. Some earrings measured 12 inches in length!

Environment

Preserving the environment is important to preserving Native American heritage. For thousands of years, Native American tribes lived completely off the land. Farming, mining, pollution have all had a part in changing native environments.

English

In the 1800s, the U.S. government built boarding schools for Indian children throughout the nation. Children were forced to leave their homes and families to live at these schools. They were required to learn English and not speak their native languages.

Epidemics

Few Indians possessed immunity to the deadly diseases, like smallpox and measles, which European explorers and settlers brought to the New World. As a result, great population loss took place. Sometimes entire tribes became extinct. Epidemics sparked by Hernando De Soto's expedition are estimated to have killed 75% of the native population in the New World.

F is for . . .

Fortunate Eagle

This colorful Native American artist is the curator and artist-in-residence of the Round House Art Gallery on the Fallon Indian Reservation. He has organized some of the most notable modern-day Indian movements. He is also an author, ceremonial leader, and historian known around the world.

Fetish

These small objects were thought to hold the spirit of an animal or a part of nature. A fetish could be an object found in nature, such as bone or wood, or it could be a carved object. The fetish was usually small enough to be carried in a small bag or on a cord. The making and use of a fetish was kept secret by its owner and only shared with the one who inherited it.

Fire Drill

A device used by Indians to make fires which consisted of a stick and a piece of wood with a tight hole in it. The stick was twirled rapidly in the hole, creating friction that would ignite shredded grass or wood powder placed nearby to start a fire.

Federal Recognition

The United States government's official acknowledgement of a group of Indians as a tribe that is eligible for government benefits, programs and funds.

Farmers

Many Nevada Indians, ancient and modern, have farming ways! Even pre-contact Indians tilled and irrigated, raising many important crops. Corn, cotton, beans, squash, melons, sunflowers, gourds, pumpkins and tobacco are all native Indian crops!

Footwear

Nevada Indians wore different footwear depending on their tribe and environment. Moccasins were made mostly of animal skin. Sandals were made of rawhide or plant material.

Family Life

Early Indian tribal life in Nevada centered around the family. Even though many family groups migrated during different seasons to obtain food, they came together several times each year for rabbit drives and festivals. During this time they feasted, danced, told stories and played games. Nevada Indians loved any excuse for a feasting day!

G is for . . .

Games

Adults played ball and other games of chance or skill. Indian children spun tops, fought pretend battles, did target-shooting, walked on stilts, played hide and seek, or competed to see who could hold their breath the longest!

Goshutes

Indians who lived in Nevada's eastern deserts and Utah's western deserts. Traveled in small family groups, hunting for any type of food. Were among the poorest of the Indians in the American Southwest. Sometimes called Diggers. However, were hard workers, even working for whites when they had the chance. Today they can be found on the Goshute Indians Reservation in Nevada and Utah.

Gens

Group of related members from different tribes.

Gathering

Native Americans gathered natural materials for food, fuel, baskets, clothing, and housing. American Indian tribes also hunted to meet basic needs. Even though some tribes planted crops, most did some kind of gathering.

Gorgets

Beautiful ornaments hung around the neck or from ears; their significance, if any, is unknown.

Gourds

Hollowed-out shell of a gourd plant's dried fruit which often grew into a specific shape. Indians raised many species of gourds. They were used for spoons, bowls, masks, rattles, and even storage.

Go To These Exciting Indian Events in Our State

AVI KWA AME Pow Wow – February, Laughlin; Snow Mountain Pow Wow – May, Snow Mountain Colony, Las Vegas; Quinn River Indian Rodeo – June, McDermitt; Reno Rodeo – June, Reno; July 4th Rodeo and Pow Wow – July, Owyhee; Traditional Fandango – July, Ely; Spirit of Wovoka Days – August, Yerington; Red Star Pow Wow – September, Reno; Pinenut Festival – September, Schurz; Pyramid Lake Rodeo – October, Nixon; LA KA LA'L BEE Pow Wow – October, Carson City; Veterans Day Pow Wow – November, Owyhee; Pahrump Valley Pow Wow – November, Pahrump; Ely Shoshone Christmas Arts and Crafts Show – November, Ely; Christmas Indian Market – December, Reno.

H is for . . .

Horn and Hooves

Indians used animal horn to make spoons and dishes. Hooves were made into rattles and bird beaks were used for decoration.

Hatchet

A small, short-handled ax, primarily used as a tool, not as a weapon. When settlers moved in, stone hatchets were replaced with iron ones.

Hair

Indians used hair as a textile. Hair from bison, mountain sheep, elk, moose, deer, dog, rabbit, beaver, or even humans were used to weave cloth, make wigs, or stuff pillows, balls, dolls or drumsticks.

Hunters

Early Indian peoples were hunters who used wooden spears with stone points to kill many kinds of large mammals that are extinct today, such as mammoths and mastodons!

Have A Nut!

The foraging lifestyle of many of Nevada's Indians made the search for food continual. One of their autumn food staples was the pine nut, also called the piñon nut.

Humboldt

Indians who once lived on Humboldt Lake in Nevada.

Horses

Spaniards brought the horse to America. At first, Indians were afraid of the horse or thought it was sacred. Later, Indians "broke" horses gently, often "hypnotizing" them with a blanket. Horses were used for transportation, trade, barter or payment. Some Indians ate horse meat in hopes of gaining the animal's power.

Hadsapoke

Indian band of Northern Paiute who once lived on the Carson River in western Nevada.

I is for . . .

Itsaatiaga

Band of Paviotso Indians that once lived near Unionville in western Nevada.

Indian Scout

This term for a guide applied to Indians or white-skinned people who served that role.

Indian Removal Act of 1830

This federal act gave President Andrew Jackson the power to relocate tribes east of the Mississippi to an "Indian Territory." The forced removal of the southeast Indians later became known as the "Trail of Tears."

Independence

Native American tribes are sovereign nations. That means they are independent. Some even issue their own passports! However, Native Americans are also considered citizens of the United States and enjoy all the rights and privileges of U.S. citizens.

Indian Wars

The U.S. War Department's official list of Indian Wars in America includes: the 1865-68 Indian Wars and the 1875 Expedition against the Indians of eastern Nevada. The Paiute, or Pyramid Lake War started in 1860 with the kidnapping of two Paiute girls.

Indian Ladder

Indians made ladders by trimming branches off a tree. Some were left at consistent intervals to provide steps.

Indian Tribes in Nevada

At one time or another, these tribes have lived in the state of Nevada: Mojave, Paiute, Shoshone, Washoe

Indian

In 1493, Christopher Columbus called the native people he met in North America "Indians" because he mistakenly believed he had sailed to India! Today, this term includes the aborigines of North and South America.

J is for . . .

Just So You Know . . .

Today you can find many Nevada Indians that follow some traditional ways. But there are also many who are entrepreneurs, doctors, lawyers, educators and even politicians! If you visit a reservation or cultural event, make sure you know visitor etiquette. Often dances are religious ceremonies and should be observed as such; religious dances should not be applauded. Photography, videotaping and drawing are all important issues - check with the tribe or individual before any is started.

Jack Wilson

Nevada Paiute Indian who became ill with a fever while working. He said he had been taken to the Great Spirit who told him if the Indians gave up white ways the earth would soon perish and come alive again only for the Indians. While he was sick, there was also a solar eclipse. The combination of Wilson's tale and the eclipse convinced many Indians that they had better follow the Great Spirit's instructions. This became the foundation for the Ghost Dance Religion that swept the Plains tribes.

Judicial Termination

Modern term to describe current efforts by various U.S. government agencies and officials (especially the judicial system) to legally decrease the sovereignty of independent Indian tribes.

Just In Time!

The Indian Arts and Crafts Act of 1990 makes it against the law to pretend that an item has been made by Native Americans if it is really not. It is illegal to offer or display for sale, or sell any art or craft product in a way that falsely suggests it is Indian produced.

Justice?

For hundreds of years, Native Americans have not received justice from federal and state governments. Native Americans have had nearly all their land taken away. Native Americans still have to fight for their rights in courts across the land.

K is for . . .

Knife

Made from various materials such as bone, reed, stone, wood, antler, shell, metal, or animal teeth (bear, beaver, etc.), knives were used as weapons but also creative handiwork.

Kill Site

An archaeological site where remains of many animals have been found along with human artifacts. Many kill sites have been useful to scientists in learning how ancient American Indians lived.

Killed Pottery

Pottery placed in a grave as an offering to the dead person was called killed pottery. A hole was formed in its base during creation. Often broken pottery was placed in a grave because Indians believed the spirit of the dead person would then be released and could travel.

Kaidatoiabie

The name of several bands of Indians that once lived in northeastern Nevada.

Knowledge

Knowledge is power. Native Americans shared knowledge with the first European settlers. Native Americans showed settlers how to plant crops, which plants were safe to eat, and other knowledge about the land.

Knots

Tied on bowstrings, spearhead and arrowhead lashings, snowshoes, and other items, knots were sometimes used to keep track of the days like a calendar—each knot equaled 1 day.

L is for . . .

Lost City

Early Puebloan/ Anasazi site, 5 miles of which was lost or is now covered by Lake Mead. Although archaeologists did not complete work on the site before Lake Mead grew behind the Hoover Dam, you can see some of the excavated artifacts at the Lost City Museum in Overton.

Leggings

Both men and women wore cloth or skin covering, which were often decorated with quills, beads, or painted designs, for their legs.

Lost Tribes of Israel

This historic theory has been floating around since 721 BC. The 10 lost tribes of Israel are supposedly groups of people gathered together by Sargon, the King of Assyria. Some say he cast out 10 of the 12 tribes of Israel. Many have tried to prove that the American Indians are these missing tribes!

Loko

Band of Northern Paiute Indians that lived near the Carson River in western Nevada.

Lodge

The term for a type of Indian house that was usually a permanent dwelling. The population of a tribe was often estimated by its number of lodges.

Land Loss

Native Americans lost their land in many ways. Conflicts with other tribes, colonization, European settlement, treaties, and removal took away Indian lands.

Lance

Spear used for hunting and war. The hunting lance had a short shaft and a broad, heavy head. The war lance was light and had a long shaft.

Lovelock Cave

Over 4,500 years ago this cave in the Humboldt Mountain Range of northern Nevada was the dwelling place of early Nevadans. At that time, the cave was located on the shore of Lake Lahontan. The people who lived here were left many artifacts. Although the culture was very advanced, it died out around 500 years ago. We do not know why.

Lariat

These throw ropes made of rawhide, buffalo hair, or horsehair sometimes measured up to 20 feet long!

M is for . . .

Maize

Also called Indian Corn. Known as a "cereal" plant because it probably began as some form of grass. The Indians in our state figured out every possible way to use corn as a food. The only thing the white man added was the creation of "corn flakes!"

Mortar and Pestle

A two-part milling tool, with a bowl-shaped stone, plus a club-shaped stone (or wooden bowl and wooden club), used for pulverizing or grinding plants or animal matter.

Movwiats

Band of Paiute that lived in southeastern Nevada in 1873.

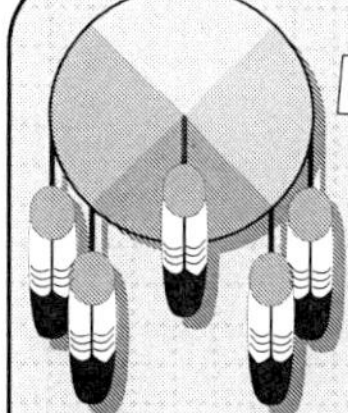

Medicine

Medicine could be good or bad. Medicines or charms were placed in a bag by young warriors and carried at all times. Some of the roots, leaves and bark that Indians in our state used as medicine are being rediscovered and used by today's doctors!

Moccasins

Indian shoes made of animal skin.

Medicine Man

A person who got the power to heal the sick through a secret means, usually from a dream or visions.

Mojave

Indian tribe that once lived along the Colorado River in Nevada. The Mojave Desert is named for the tribe. They built two different dwellings - one for warm weather, another for cold weather. They did hunt, fish and gather some, but they were primarily farmers. They traveled from the area around the present-day borders of Arizona, California and Nevada to the Gulf of California on trading trips. The Mojave were known as fierce fighters. War parties had 3 groups - archers, clubbers and stickmen.

N is for . . .

Nation

There are many Indian nations located within the United States, such as the Washoe Nation. Indian nations are called nations because their governments and laws are independent of and separate from the U.S. government. The federal government must have "government to government" relations with these Indian nations, just as it would with foreign nations, like England or Spain.

Nomadic

A way of life in which people frequently moved from one location to another in search of food. "Seminomadic" people had permanent villages, but left them in certain seasons to hunt, fish, or gather wild plant foods.

Numaga, Chief

Northern Paiute Indian leader at the Paiute War at Pyramid Lake, and nephew of Winnemucca.

November

In 1990, President George Bush approved a joint resolution designating November 1990 "National American Indian Heritage Month." Similar proclamations have been issued each year since 1994.

Names

Indian names were often changed during one's lifetime. These names could be derived from events that happened during the person's birth, childhood, adolescence, war service, or retirement from active tribal life. Some names came from dreams, some were inherited, and sometimes names were stolen or taken in revenge. Today some Indians maintain old, traditional Indian names, while others take modern names. Since settlers often did not read or write Indian languages, they recorded Indian names phonetically (as they "sounded"). Thus Indian names were often misspelled.

National Museum of the American Indian

The Smithsonian's National Museum of the American Indian on the National Mall in Washington, D.C., symbolizes a deeper understanding between America's first citizens and those who have come to make these shores their home.

National Indian Housing Improvement Council

Located in Carson City, Nevada. Founded in 1974. Provides support to tribal housing agencies in an effort to provide safe and affordable housing for Native people in American Indian communities and Alaska Native villages.

O is for . . .

Old Bones

No one knows for sure when the first people came to North America, but scientists have dated bones and artifacts discovered at Clovis, New Mexico around 11,200 years old. Testing on a skeleton found on the Channel Islands, off the coast of California showed they were about 13,000 years old. And, evidence of human habitation in southern New Mexico suggests that people may have been there as far back as 38,000 years ago.

Origins

Some scientists believe that Native Americans actually came across a land bridge between Asia and North America. They say that during an ice age thousands of years ago, the water level was much lower and people could have walked between the two continents.

Old Winnemucca

Paiute chief who opposed fighting whites because he believe it would only make them more determined to conquer the Indian and take their lands. He was right.

Oil

Indians extracted oil from the many layers of fat that came with fresh bear meat. The fat was boiled down in earthen pots to produce the oil, which was stored in gourds and pots. The oil was used for cooking and even beautifying the body! Indians would mix red pigment with the oil, add the fragrances of cinnamon and sassafras, and rub it all over their bodies.

Orators

Many Indian leaders were excellent public speakers. Powerful and dramatic speakers were vital to leaders who wanted to influence their tribe. Watch for famous Indian quotations in literature and textbooks!

Office of Indian Education Programs

This is a service organization devoted to providing quality education opportunities for American Indian people. Established in the latter part of the nineteenth century to carry out the federal government's education commitment to Indian tribes, it has become the only national education system for American Indian children and adults.

P is for . . .

Powwow

The original form of the word meant "medicine man." Medicine men would often use noise motion and confusion to scare away harmful spirits and cure people. It was also a gathering to talk about political matters. Today, the powwow is an event where Indians gather to sing, perform ceremonial dances, and share cultural pride and traditions.

Petroglyph Park

Located near Grimes Point; see ancient Indian art from past civilizations here!

Paiute

Name may mean "Water Ute" or "True Ute." The Northern Paiute lived in western Nevada and considered more warlike; the Southern Paiute lived in the southern part of the state and were often called Diggers. Both groups were nomadic hunters and gatherers, and have reservations in Nevada today.

Paint

Indians used many natural materials to make paint, like clay mixed with oil or grease. Yellow "paint" was made with the gall bladder of a buffalo! Why did they paint their faces or bodies? Indians used paint to look scary or beautiful, to disguise themselves, or to protect their skin from sunburn or insect bites. Indians often applied red paint because it symbolized strength and success. That is why settlers often referred to the Indians as Red Men.

Pogaits

Paiute band that lived near Colville; name means "fish eaters."

Pueblo Grande de Nevada

What is commonly called the "Lost City." Thousands of Puebloans and Anasazi once lived here. But around A.D. 1150 they left their homes and fields without a trace. The "Lost City" was made up of pithouses, campsites, salt mines, caves, and single story adobe dwellings.

Papoose

An American Indian infant aged between birth and one year is called a papoose. A papoose spent most of his or her days snugly wrapped in a kind of cradle made of skins or bark and a wooden frame that hung on the mother's back. This sturdy frame also allowed a mother to lean her papoose against a tree or rock within sight as she worked.

Picture History

Some Indians kept a record of time and important events by painting or drawing pictures or symbols on skin, bark, or stone.

Pottery

Indian pottery was made from built-up spirals of clay that were molded or paddled, or a combination of the two methods. Most pottery served as cooking vessels.

Q is for . . .

Quillwork

Indians used the quills of porcupine or birds to make a type of embroidery. Quills were dyed with juice from berries and other materials. When they were ready to be used, the quills were either mashed with teeth or softened with hot water and flattened with rocks. The quills were then laced into moccasins, shirts, pipe covers, and other items. Beads which Indians received by trading with settlers eventually replaced quillwork.

Quality

Native American arts and crafts are known for their excellent craftsmanship and striking designs. This work is often influenced by things found in nature especially plants and animals.

Quiver

Case used to hold arrows; made of woven plant materials or animal skins.

Quarry Site

A location where Indians went for workable stone such as flint and made stone tools.

Quirt

A short riding whip with a wood, bone, or horn handle.

R is for . . .

Rain Dancing

The rain dance ceremony, performed to encourage rainfall, was common among Indian religions because good weather is vital for a successful harvest. Rainmakers were in tune with nature; there are actual reported cases of Indians producing or preventing rain!

Roots

Indians used plant roots for food, medicine, dye, baskets, cloth, rope, salt, flavoring, and just to chew!

Rattles

Indians of Nevada made rattles from bird beaks, animal hooves, bones, pods, seashells, turtle shells and other animal parts. The rattles are used in ceremonies.

Religion

Nevada Indians believed in a peaceful spirit world where the dead kept watch over the living. They also believed in the special powers of nature which existed in mountains, lakes, wind, fog and animals.

Rawhide

Untanned animal hide. The "green" hide was stretched on the ground or over a frame. Flesh and fat were removed. The skin was dried, washed, then buried with wood ashes which made the hair come off. Used by the Nevada Indian to make drumheads, lash lodge poles, mend broken objects and in many other ways.

Reservations

The U.S. government set aside, or "reserved," land for the Indians. These reservations originally served as a sort of prison during the beginning stages of Indian removal. At that time, reservations provided the government with some control over Indian activity and residency. This land was usually considerably less desirable land than the Indians' native territories. Today's reservations are lands that are tribally held, yet protected by the government.

Removal

One of the U.S. government policies of the late 1800s regarding the "Indian Problem" in the west was to remove Indians from their native homelands and consolidate them with other tribes onto reservations. Another policy was to turn an extremely small part of their homelands into a reservation to contain them.

S is for . . .

Sign Language

A way for Indians to communicate with others from a tribe whose language they did not speak.

Shaman

Medicine man and spiritual leader who was supposed to have special healing power from another world.

Secret Societies

Indians had secret groups, usually organized for religious or ceremonial reasons. Each society had a purpose, such as to cure disease.

Shield

A piece of "armor" made of a rawhide-covered frame, which was carried into battle. Shields also could be decorative and religious objects. Many tribes make shields today as an art form!

Sweatlodge

Structure used for ritual purification by sweating from exposure to very hot fires or hot steam from pouring water over hot stones. Also called a sweathouse, for some tribes also doubling as clubhouses.

Stone-boiling

Cooking method by placing preheated stones into cooking vessels.

Sacred Bundles

A group of objects treasured by a tribe. They were well-guarded and often taken into battle. The items were publicly shown only on very important occasions.

Shoshone

Indian tribe that once lived in many northwestern states, including Nevada. Also known as the Snakes or Snake Nation, possibly from their sign language for salmon, or from the Snake River. The Western Shoshone were the branch that lived in central and eastern Nevada. Lived in brush shelters and foraged for food. Today they can be found on several reservations in Nevada.

Shoshoko

The part of the Shoshone tribe that did not have horses and so were called "walkers."

Stewart Indian Museum

Located on the campus of the former Stewart Indian Boarding School. Some buildings of this intertribal school were constructed by stone masons and students between 1923 and 1957. The school opened in 1890 and closed in 1980. It was originally called the Carson Indian Training School, but later renamed for the senator who got federal funding to keep the school open.

Shivwits

Indian band that was moved to a reservation in Nevada in 1873.

T is for . . .

Tobacco
A sacred plant early Indians used to make offering to their gods, cure diseases, bring good luck, seal agreements and bind treaties.

Treaties
Written agreements between the U. S. government and the Indians, most of which involved the Indians giving up their native lands.

Throwing Stick
A sling or grooved stick used to hurl a lance or spear. It was used by Nevada Indians before bows and arrows.

Totem
The spirit of some natural object (usually an animal) taken by an Indian, tribe or family to guard over them.

Tomahawk
A club, axe or hammer used to chop wood, drive stakes in the ground or as a weapon.

Thom, Melvin
A Walker River Paiute from Nevada who helped found the National Indian Youth Council in 1961. He was also it's first president. The NIYC is the second oldest American Indian organization.

Tracking
To follow a trail by finding a sign such as a broken blade of grass, a moved stone or moccasin track. Indians learned to trail as children, so that they could find food, track enemies and disguise their own signs.

Teeth
Nevada Indians hung teeth on cords to make necklaces.

Tavibo
Paiute chief and shaman. When the white men were pushing his people off their native lands, he said he had a vision in which all people would be swallowed by a giant earthquake. Only the Indian would return to a land of plenty. Many of his followers hoped his vision would come to pass. Died around 1870.

Tribe
A group of Indians with shared culture, history, original territory, ancestry, social organization, and governmental structure. A tribe may contain several bands of Indians.

Thunderbird
A mythological Indian figure, as well as a part of the constellations for many Indians. Thunderbird mythology is mostly different from tribe to tribe, in general either coexisting with ancestors as an actual bird, or appearing as a spiritual nature god. The Thunderbird was good to the people in either case. Much mythology ties the thunderbird with thunder, lightning and storms.

U is for . . .

U.S. Bureau of Indian Affairs

Provides public services such as law enforcement, land records, economic development, and education to Indians. Known for mismanagement and ethical problems.

U.S. Army

Many Native Americans have fought bravely for the United States Army. Many have also given their lives for a country that was not always accepting of them.

Unique

Each and every tribe has its own unique customs, language, and traditions.

U.S. Indian Schools

The Bureau of Indian Affairs operates hundreds of federal schools around the nation. Enrollment of Native American children measures in the thousands!

U.S. Indian Reorganization Act

Passed by Congress in 1934, the act authorized Indian tribes to establish and conduct their own governments, and to form businesses.

U.S. President

Once called Great White Father by Indians.

U.S. Colonists

Called Long Knives or Big Knives by early Indians, who also called English explorers "Coat Men."

U.S. Indian Wars

The U.S. War Department has compiled an official list of "Indian Wars" that occurred in the United States. Over 50 wars were fought between the U.S. and the Indians during the period of 1790-1850.

V is for . . .

Vessels

Indians carried water in special gourds shaped liked bottles, called water vessels.

Village Councils

These were held in the town (council) house and occurred to discuss and decide important matters. Harmony and agreement was essential to tribal unity. Rather than vote on issues, they were discussed until everyone was satisfied. Anyone who wanted to could speak freely. Everyone did not always agree on the outcome, but everyone avoided conflict by pushing their case.

Vegetable Dyes

Indians could not buy color from the store like we can today. Instead, they created many different colors from the things they found on earth like plants, flowers, shrubs, trees, roots, and berries. They made beautiful and unique reds, oranges, yellows, greens, browns, and violets. These dyes were used for baskets, pottery, weaving, body makeup, and clothing.

Very Hungry

There were Indians who here hunters, gatherers and foragers, that often ate whatever they could find! How hungry would you have to be to eat what they sometimes ate: reptiles, larvae, and insects?

Villages

Many Nevada Indians lived in villages! Villages were formed around different clans or bands within the tribe, but could also contain different clans living together. Villages were usually permanent settlements, although semi-nomadic tribes have been known to migrate between permanent villages.

Valley of Fire State Park

Site of petroglyphs that the Anasazi and Paiute peoples many have used as maps, clan records, or a lost language.

W is for . . .

War Bonnet
Special headdress worn into battle, often adorned with feathers.

War Pony
Horse, often painted with colorful paint and ridden into battle.

Wickiup
Brush shelter or mat-covered house with a stick frame. Primarily built by the Paiute, Shoshone, and other tribes of Nevada.

War Dance
Indian braves danced this before going into battle. The dance was a way of assembling the braves and getting them to commit to the fight ahead.

Washoe
Indian tribe that once lived in the areas of the Truckee River and Lake Tahoe in western Nevada and eastern California. Today their land is made up of a group of allotments, colonies, and the Washoe Ranch.

Walker-Bonneville Party
In 1833-34 Joseph Walker and around 40 men left this exploration expedition and crossed the salt flats of Utah into Nevada. Near the Humboldt Sink, they met about 800 Northern Paiutes. Most of these Indians had never seen firearms. A fight erupted and the white men killed 30 or 40 Indians. The rest of the Paiutes fled in terror. This was the first large-scale battle between Indians and whites in our state.

Whistle
Indians from Nevada made them from the wing bones of birds. The whistles made the sound of the bird the bones came from! Used to communicate, signal, sound an alarm or even flirt with a maiden!

War Club
A weapon made of stone, bone, or wood in the shape of a club.

White Man
Indians generally called them Pale Face, a name the white men themselves suggested!

Winnemucca, Sarah
Paiute woman born in Nevada around 1844. Was an interpreter and teacher at an Indian school near Lovelock, which she had managed to obtain lands for. Died around 1891.

XYZ are for . . .

Xenophobe

A xenophobe is someone who is afraid of foreign people, their customs and cultures, or foreign things. Many of the first European settlers were afraid of Native American cultures.

You Bet!

Some Native Americans say that Casinos make a lot of money. Others say that too many people have a gambling problem. In the 1980s and 1990s, many tribes discussed whether or not gambling casinos should be allowed. Now that many casinos have been built across the country, the debate has switched to how it should be controlled.

Zounds!

Between 1871 and 1913, at least 98 traditional agreements between tribes and the United States were negotiated and 96 of them were ratified by Congress. Each agreement remains as law (unless changed by a later agreement)!

ZZZZZZ...

Shamans and medicine men were not the only people who had access to the spirit world. Indians believed that people could make contact with spirits every night in their dreams! Dreamers could travel back to the time of man's creation or far ahead into their own futures. They also believed that dreams contained warnings or commands from the spirits. Many tribes felt that they had to act out their dreams as soon as they awoke. If an Indian dreamed about bathing, for example, he would run to his neighbors' houses first thing in the morning, and his neighbors would throw kettles full of cold water over him.

Y... Or, "Why?"

1. Why do you think Indian warriors carried charms with them? Some Indian medicines have been scientifically proven to have true healing power and are still used today. Do you think their charms had any real power to help them win battles?
2. Why do you think the American government kept relocating Indians onto reservations and then making the reservations smaller and smaller?
3. Why did Indians use items such as a pipe in ceremonies? What kinds of symbolic objects do we use in ceremonies today?
4. Why and how did Indians use natural materials in creative ways?
5. Many Indian tribes are running successful businesses on their reservations today. There is one industry that many tribes are making a lot of money at. Do you know what this is? Hint: "I'll bet you do!"

Which Famous Native American Am I?

Solve the puzzle!

Word Bank

Black Elk	Crazy Horse	Sitting Bull	Sequoia
Sacajawea	Chief Joseph	Geronimo	Pocahontas

Down

1. This Shoshone woman joined Lewis and Clark as their guide and translator and helped make the expedition a success! Hint: She has 4 "a"s in her name!
4. This man gave the Cherokee their first alphabet so that they could write. Until then, they communicated only by speaking and drawing pictures. Hint: A famous ancient tree also has the same name!
5. He was one of the fiercest of Indian warriors! He fought against white settlers in Arizona and New Mexico to keep his people from being pushed off their lands. Hint: Jump!

Across

2. A legend says that this brave Algonquian woman saved the life of Englishman John Smith. Hint: Disney produced a movie about her.
3. He fought at Little Bighorn when he was only 13! He was also a wise "shaman" who saw visions and could advise people. Hint: Part of his name is an animal with antlers!
6. He was a great Sioux warrior who won the battle against General Custer at Little Bighorn in 1876. Hint: His horse was not crazy!
7. A leader of the Lakota (Sioux) tribe who lived on the Standing Rock Reservation in North Dakota after the battle of Little Bighorn. He tried to make conditions better for his people there, so the U.S. government called him a "troublemaker." Hint: He did not sit all the time!
8. A wise and brave chief of the Nez Percé who tried to bring his people to Canada to escape war. He said, "From where the sun now stands, I will fight no more forever." Hint: His father's name was "Old Joseph."

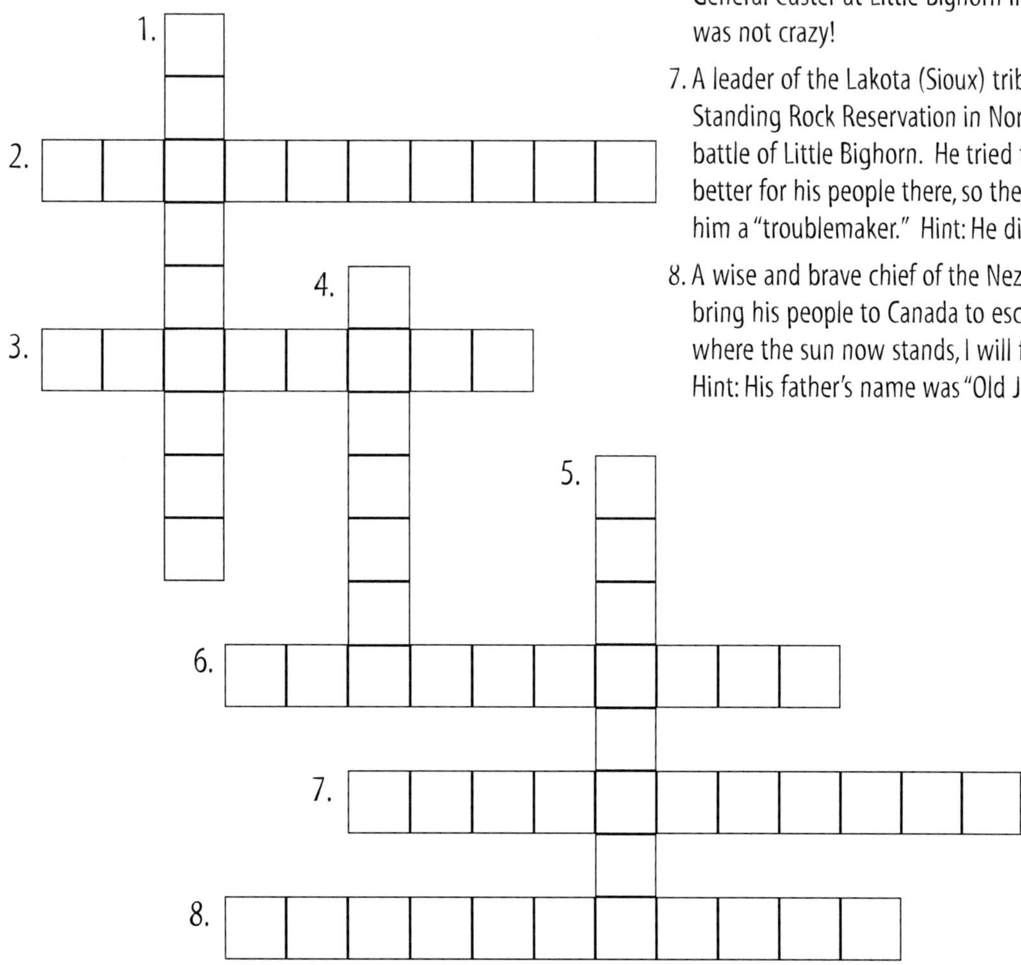

Answer Key: 1. Sacajawea; 2. Pocahontas; 3. Black Elk; 4. Sequoia; 5. Geronimo; 6. Crazy Horse; 7. Sitting Bull; 8. Chief Joseph

Different Ways for Different Indians!

North American Indian tribes are divided into different areas. In each of these areas, tribes shared common ways of living with each other. They might make similar arts or crafts, they might eat the same foods, or they might have had the same beliefs. These activities are all part of their "culture." Each area had its own culture, which was different from the tribes in all the other areas.

Below is a map of all the different groups of Indian tribes in North America. Color each area with a different color. You will see a colorful picture of how Native Americans can all be called "Indians" but still have very different cultures!

Celebration!

Powwows are big festivals where Native Americans gather to sing, dance, and eat together. It is a time to celebrate and show pride in their culture. Powwows can last from one afternoon to several days. The Indians dress in native costumes and dance ancient dances to the beating of drums.

Artists sell their arts and crafts. You might be able to buy some real Native American food cooked on an open fire. Native Americans go to powwows to be with each other, share ideas, and just have fun! Most powwows are also open to people who are not Indian. It's a great place to learn about Native American culture!

If you went to a powwow this weekend, what do you think you would see? What do you think might NOT be there? Circle the objects you think you would see at a powwow. Put an X through those you probably won't see.

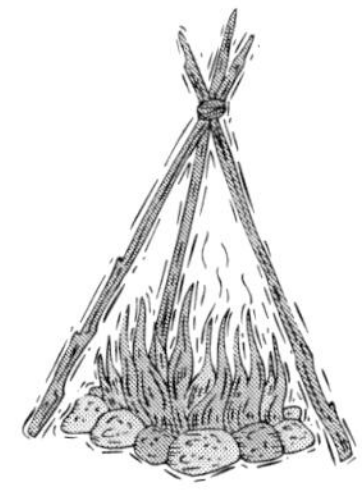

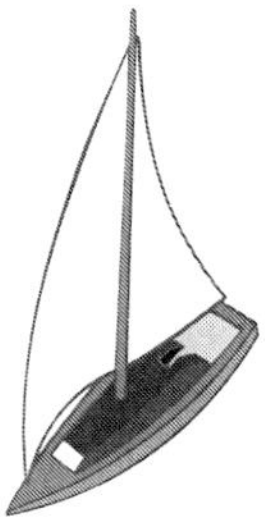

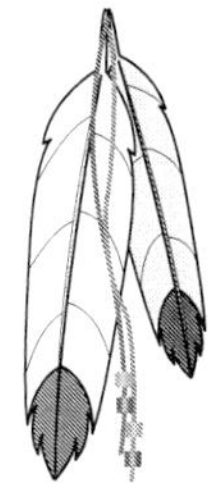

Answer Key: Circled objects are: beads, moccasins, open fire, drums, feathers, baskets, kids, food, drums, horse.

Make an Indian Weaving!

Many Native Americans used weaving to create useful things like sashes (belts), bags, mats, and blankets. They used animal hair to make yarn, and dyed the yarn with natural dyes from fruits and other plants. They also used some plant fibers, like cotton, to make weaving thread.

Weave a small Native American mat of your own. Use different colors of yarn to create a beautiful pattern in your weaving. Place a favorite object on the mat or hang it on your wall!

Prepare the "loom"

Cut a piece of cardboard 5 inches wide and 6 inches long. Along the two 5-inch sides (the "short" sides), have an adult cut slits 1/4 inch deep. These slits should be 1/2 inch apart from each other. So, on each short side you will have 9 slits.

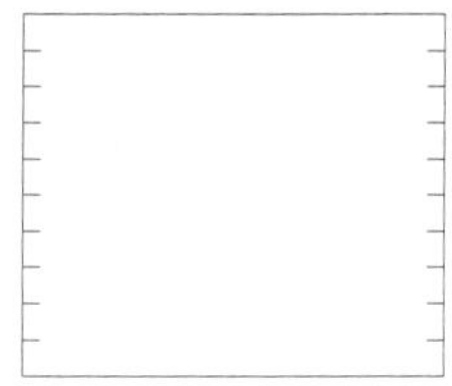

Directions:

1. Take a long piece of yarn and bring it from the back through the first slit (the one next to the edge of the cardboard.) The end of the yarn will hang down behind the cardboard.

2. Bring the yarn right across the front of the cardboard to the slit opposite the one your yarn came through.

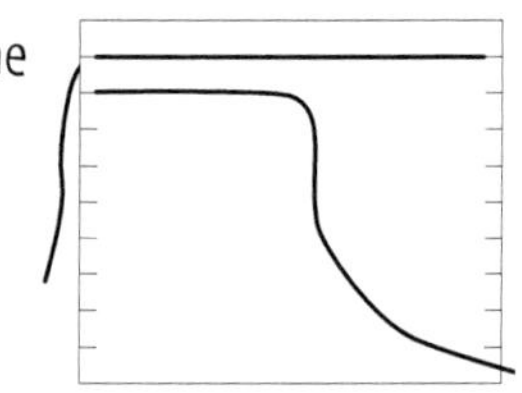

3. Now bring the yarn under the back of the cardboard and then up again through the second slit.

4. Repeat #2 and #3, until you have 9 strands of yarn across the front of your cardboard!

5. Then cut the yarn and tie the two loose ends in the back of the cardboard.

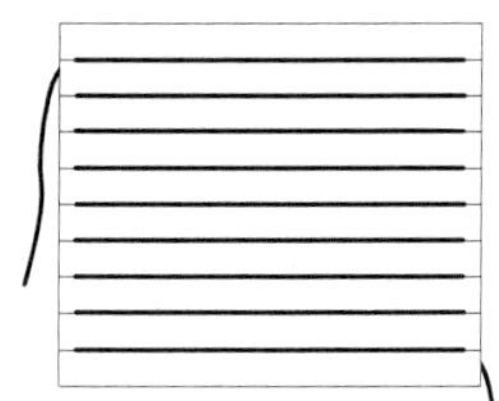

6. Take another piece of yarn and start feeding it through the 9 strands, going over one, under the next over the next, etc. When you get to the end, pull the yarn behind the cardboard and around to the front, and begin again. This time, whatever strand you went over, go under. And whatever strand you went under, go over.

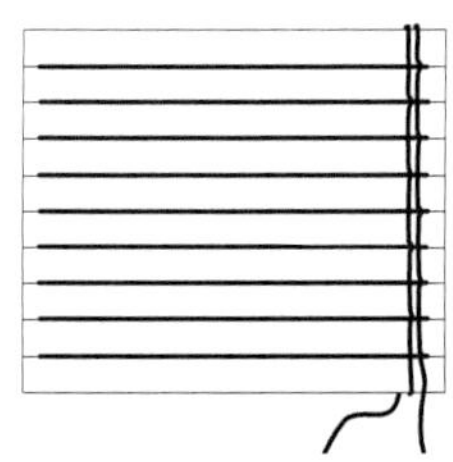

7. Repeat this pattern until the front of your cardboard in covered. Then cut the yarn in the back of the cardboard, and trim it to create a fringe for your mat!

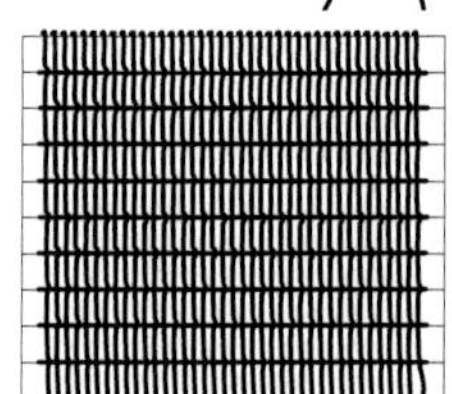

Tips:

- For a wild look, use variegated or different colored yarn!
- For a tighter mat, push the under/over strands up against the previous strands during weaving.
- To keep your mat from unravelling, tie neighboring fringe together up close to the mat.

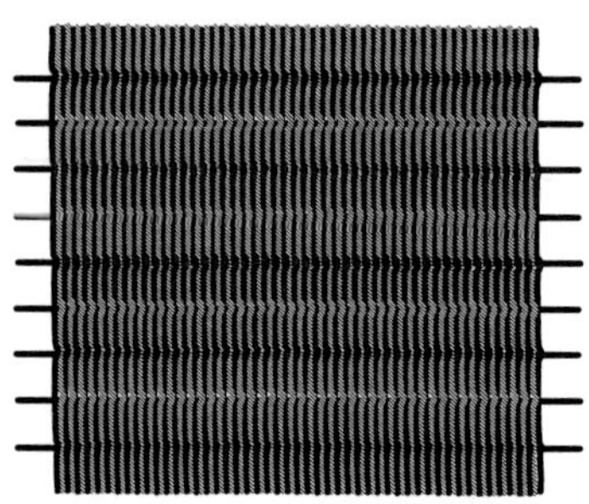

Finders Keepers?

Native Americans have many buried treasures. For hundreds of years, special objects would sometimes be buried with Native Americans, or maybe they would just be lost. Archeologists used to dig for interesting artifacts in old Native American gravesites. They would keep the Native American bones or the arrowheads, rattles, masks and other objects that they found. But this made the Native Americans feel like they were being robbed.

In 1990, the U.S. government passed a law that said that no one could look for or take these Native American objects anymore. And whoever had any already had to give them back to the people they belonged to. This is called repatriation

Help the archeologist return the artifact to a Native American.

Fast Fact

An artifact is an object that was made by people a long time ago for some useful purpose.

Busy Hands!

Before modern times, Native Americans didn't have stores where they went to buy things. They made everything they needed.

What did Indians make with their own hands? Use the Word Bank and pictures to find out!

Word Bank

blanket	moccasins	arrows	pottery	canoe
mat	food	jewelry	pouch	box

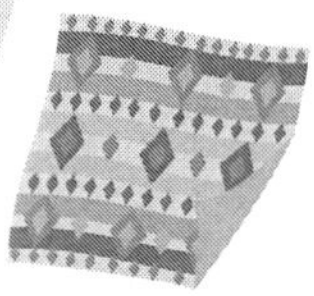 ___ ___ ___

 ___ ___ ___ ___

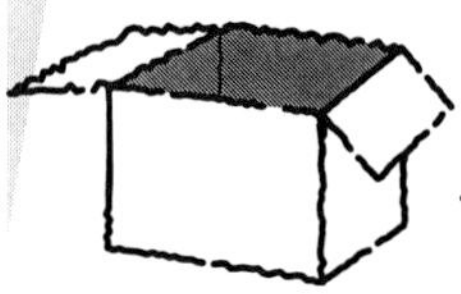 ___ ___ ___

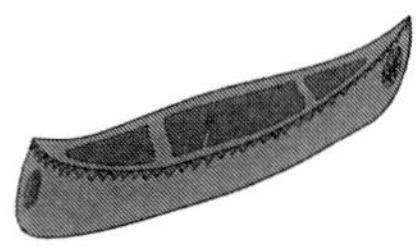 ___ ___ ___ ___ ___

 ___ ___ ___ ___ ___ ___ ___

 ___ ___ ___ ___ ___

 ___ ___ ___ ___ ___ ___ ___ ___ ___ ___

 ___ ___ ___ ___ ___ ___

 ___ ___ ___ ___ ___ ___ ___

 ___ ___ ___ ___ ___ ___ ___

American Indians Today

Beginning with the first letter of each group of letters, cross out every other letter to discover some new words. You may not have heard of these before, but you can read all about them!

1. Many Indians live on these, but many more do not!

TRYELSDEBRNVJAOTPIPOWNASX

____

2. Many Indians have been poor for a long time because for many years the government took away their lands and their ability to make a living.

TPKOOVWEBRNTXYA

____

3. Many Indians have been studying hard at school and going to college in order to earn more money. Education helps the Indians make their lives better. These Native Americans are working to become:

TSJUMCBCFEYSMSOFPUVL

____

4. This is a big term that means Native Americans have worked hard to get the U.S. government to let them rule themselves. This means that they have their own laws and make their own decisions. They are like a separate country inside the U.S.! Now, try and see if you can get your parents to give you the same thing!

TSGENLBF **JDGEETSEWRAMCIHNUAKTYIKOTNU**

______________ ______________________________

Fast Fact

What do Indians work as today?

- doctors
- nurses
- factory workers
- artists
- lawyers
- actors

The same kinds of jobs any American might work at!

Native Americans Move to the City!

Solve the code to discover the mystery words!

A	B	C	D	E	F	G	H	I	J	K	L	M
✷	❀	⌘	♣	➧	♥	❢	✰	✂	✆	☛	✈	✉
N	**O**	**P**	**Q**	**R**	**S**	**T**	**U**	**V**	**W**	**X**	**Y**	**Z**
✿	✩	❖	✡	✐	❥	☎	✒	✙	✖	✍	✠	✓

1. During the 1950s and 1960s, the American government paid Indians to leave their homes on reservations and move to cities to get jobs. If cities are sometimes called urban areas, then these brave Indians were called:

___ ___ ___ ___ ___ ___ ___ ___ ___ ___ ___ ___

✒ ✐ ❀ ✷ ✿ ✂ ✿ ♣ ✂ ✷ ✿ ❥

2. Many Indians chose to stay on their reservations and not move to the city. They thought that if they moved to the city, they would lose the way of life that their parents and ancestors had taught. These Indians called themselves:

___ ___ ___ ___ ___ ___ ___ ___ ___ ___ ___ ___ ___ ___ ___ ___ ___ ___

✐ ➧ ❥ ➧ ✐ ✙ ✷ ☎ ✂ ✩ ✿ ✂ ✿ ♣ ✂ ✷ ✿ ❥

3. Native Americans who moved to cities lived close to each other. They tried to keep their way of life as much as possible. They did not want to forget their religion, native art, or music. They did not want to lose their:

___ ___ ___ ___ ___ ___ ___

⌘ ✒ ✈ ☎ ✒ ✐ ➧

4. Are you afraid of heights? Many people are. The Mohawk Indians are not! Many of them work hundreds of feet above the city to build steel frames for skyscrapers. People who do this work above the city are:

___ ___ ___ ___ ___ ___ ___ ___ ___ ___ ___ ___

❥ ☎ ➧ ➧ ✈ ✖ ✩ ✐ ☛ ➧ ✐ ❥

5. Today urban Indians and reservation Indians come together to celebrate their culture. They share ideas and stories. They dance and beat drums. They make and sell Indian jewelry. During these celebrations, Indians remember how much they have to be proud of! These big parties are called

___ ___ ___ ___ ___ ___ ___

❖ ✩ ✖ ✖ ✩ ✖ ❥

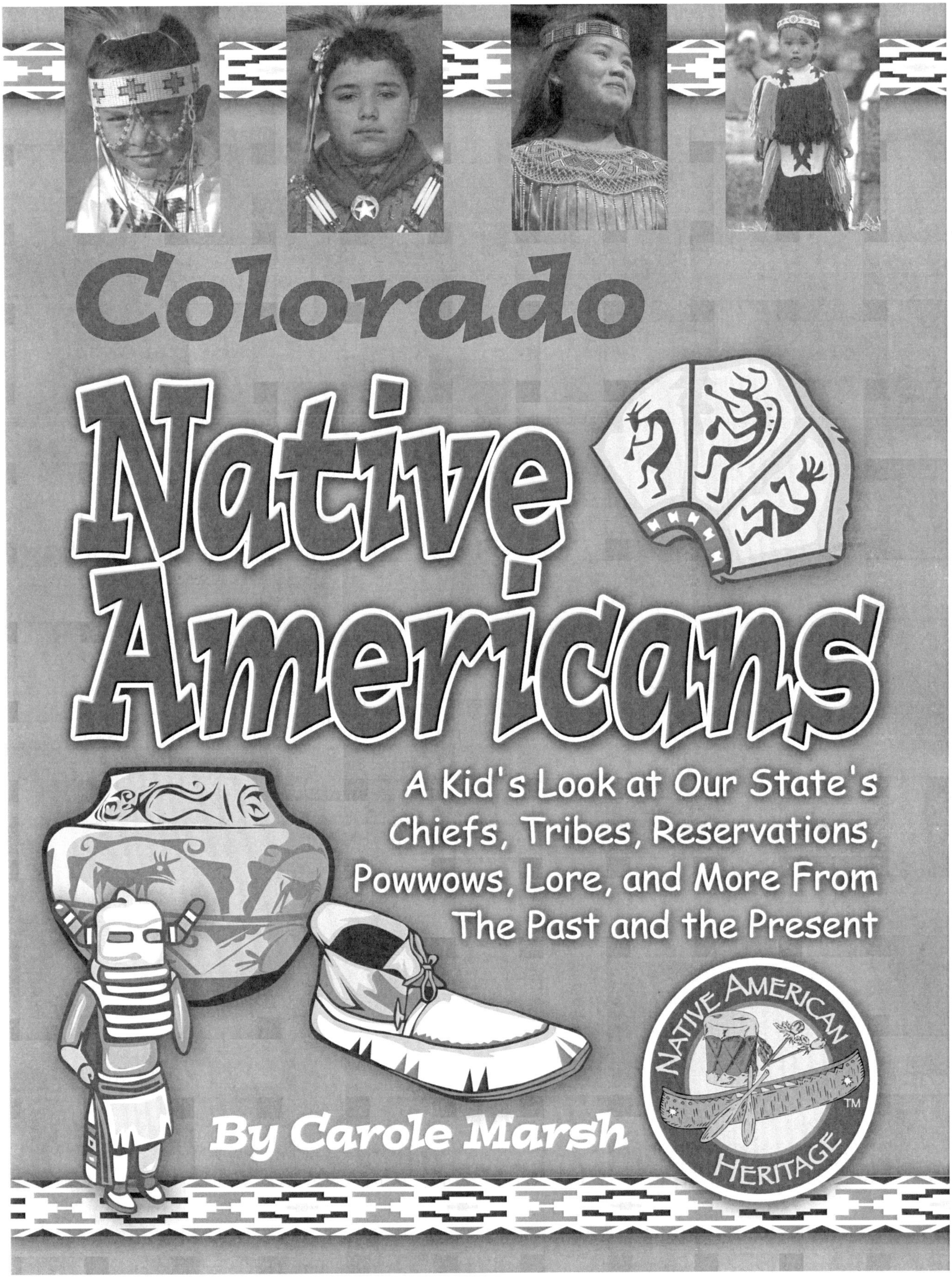

Graphic Design: Lynette Rowe • Cover Design: Victoria DeJoy

NATIVE AMERICAN HERITAGE™

CAROLE MARSH BOOKS

Published by
GALLOPADE™
INTERNATIONAL
800-536-2GET
www.gallopade.com

Gallopade is proud to be a member of these educational organizations and associations:

The National School Supply and Equipment Association (NSSEA)
American Booksellers Association (ABA)
Virginia Educational Media Association (VEMA)
Association of Partners for Public Lands (APPL)
Museum Store Association (MSA)
National Association for Gifted Children (NAGC)
Publishers Marketing Association (PMA)
International Reading Association (IRA)
Association of African American Museums (AAAM)